Dear Parent:

Congratulations! Your child is taking the first steps on an exciting journey. The destination? Independent reading!

STEP INTO READING® will help your child get there. The program offers books at five levels that accompany children from their first attempts at reading to reading success. Each step includes fun stories, fiction and nonfiction, and colorful art. There are also Step into Reading Sticker Books, Step into Reading Math Readers, and Step into Reading Phonics Readers— a complete literacy program with something to interest every child.

Learning to Read, Step by Step!

Ready to Read Preschool–Kindergarten
• big type and easy words • rhyme and rhythm • picture clues
For children who know the alphabet and are eager to begin reading.

Reading with Help Preschool–Grade 1
• basic vocabulary • short sentences • simple stories
For children who recognize familiar words and sound out new words with help.

Reading on Your Own Grades 1–3
• engaging characters • easy-to-follow plots • popular topics
For children who are ready to read on their own.

Reading Paragraphs Grades 2–3
• challenging vocabulary • short paragraphs • exciting stories
For newly independent readers who read simple sentences with confidence.

Ready for Chapters Grades 2–4
• chapters • longer paragraphs • full-color art
For children who want to take the plunge into chapter books but still like colorful pictures.

STEP INTO READING® is designed to give every child a successful reading experience. The grade levels are only guides. Children can progress through the steps at their own speed, developing confidence in their reading, no matter what their grade.

Remember, a lifetime love of reading starts with a single step!

Copyright © 2000, 2003 Disney Enterprises, Inc. Based on the "Winnie the Pooh" works by
A. A. Milne and E. H. Shepard. All rights reserved under International and Pan-American
Copyright Conventions. Published in the United States by Random House Children's Books, a
division of Random House, Inc., New York, and simultaneously in Canada by Random House
of Canada Limited, Toronto, in conjunction with Disney Enterprises, Inc. Originally published
in different form by Disney Press in 2000.

www.stepintoreading.com

Educators and librarians, for a variety of teaching tools, visit us at
www.randomhouse.com/teachers

Library of Congress Cataloging-in-Publication Data
Gaines, Isabel.
I love you, Mama / by Isabel Gaines ; illustrated by Mark Marderosian and Fred Marvin.
    p.   cm. — (Step into reading. A step 2 book)
SUMMARY: Winnie the Pooh, Tigger, and Roo plan a surprise Mother's Day party for Kanga, but
Roo is unable to find the right present.
ISBN 0-7364-2091-6 (trade) — ISBN 0-7364-8018-8 (lib. bdg.)
[1. Mother's Day—Fiction. 2. Gifts—Fiction. 3. Parties—Fiction. 4. Toys—Fiction.]
I. Marderosian, Mark, ill.   II. Marvin, Fred, ill.   III. Title.   IV. Step into reading. Step 2 book.
PZ7.G1277 Ik 2003b [E]—dc21   2002013676

Printed in the United States of America 11 10 9 8 7 6

STEP INTO READING, RANDOM HOUSE, and the Random House colophon are registered trademarks
of Random House, Inc.

Disney
Winnie the Pooh

I Love You, Mama!

Adapted by Isabel Gaines
Illustrated by Mark Marderosian
and Fred Marvin

Random House 🏠 New York

One day,
Tigger and Roo
were out bouncing.

They bounced up to
Christopher Robin.

"Hello!" said Tigger
and Roo.
"Hi!" said
Christopher Robin.

"Tomorrow is
Mother's Day,"
said Christopher Robin.

"Yay!" said Roo.

"I want to give Mama

a surprise."

"Tiggers love surprises!"
said Tigger.
"So do mothers!"
said Roo.

Christopher Robin
had an idea.
"We can have
a surprise party,"
he said.

All the friends
got together.
They planned
the party.

The next morning, Roo
remembered something.
He had forgotten to get
Mama a present.

Roo looked for
something to give Mama.
But he only had toys.

Roo heard a knock
at the front door.
He ran out of his room.
It was time
for the party.

Kanga opened the door.
"HAPPY MOTHER'S DAY!"
everyone shouted.

"Thank you!"

Kanga said.

"Sit in your
favorite chair, Mama!"
said Roo.

"Time for presents!"
said Roo.

18

Eeyore gave Kanga
some droopy flowers.

"Tigger has something,
too," said Roo.

Tigger gave Kanga
a bouncy bunch
of flowers.

"My flowers are not
as nice as Tigger's,"
said Eeyore.
"Your flowers are
pretty, too,"
said Kanga.

Christopher Robin

gave out

homemade muffins.

Rabbit gave Kanga
vegetables from
his garden.

Piglet gave Kanga
a big cake.

Pooh gave her
a pot of honey.

"Now Owl will say
a poem," said Roo.

"Kanga is a mother
unlike any other.
She cares for us all
even when we fall,"
said Owl.

Kanga clapped.

Owl took a bow.

It was Roo's turn.

But he did not have

a gift for Kanga.

He started to cry.

"I forgot to get you

a present," he said.

"But I already
have the best
present ever,"
said Kanga.

"You do?" asked Roo.

"Yes!" said Kanga.

"I have <u>you</u>!"